PIGS ON THE FARM/
CERDOS DE GRANJA

By Rose Carraway

Traducción al español: Eduardo Alamán

Gareth Stevens
Publishing

Please visit our website, www.garethstevens.com. For a free color catalog of all our high-quality books, call toll free 1-800-542-2595 or fax 1-877-542-2596.

Library of Congress Cataloging-in-Publication Data

Carraway, Rose.
[Pigs on the farm. English & Spanish]
Pigs on the farm = Cerdos de granja / Rose Carraway.
   p. cm. — (Farm animals = Animales de granja)
Includes index.
ISBN 978-1-4339-7402-1 (library binding)
1. Swine—Juvenile literature. I. Title. II. Title: Cerdos de granja.
SF395.5.C3718 2013
599.63'3—dc23

                     2011052951

First Edition

Published in 2013 by
Gareth Stevens Publishing
111 East 14th Street, Suite 349
New York, NY 10003

Copyright © 2013 Gareth Stevens Publishing

Editor: Katie Kawa
Designer: Andrea Davison-Bartolota
Spanish Translation: Eduardo Alamán

Photo credits: Cover, p. 1 Ppaauullee/Shutterstock.com; p. 5 © iStockphoto.com/Kay Ransom; pp. 7, 11, 17, 19, 23 (bottom), 24 (straw) iStockphoto/Thinkstock; p. 9 © iStockphoto.com/James Pauls; p. 13 © iStockphoto.com/ Craig W. Walsh; p. 15 hvoya/Shutterstock.com; pp. 21, 24 Uwe Pillat/Shutterstock.com; pp. 23 (top), 24 (tail) Tsekhmister/Shutterstock.com.

Printed in the United States of America

CPSIA compliance information: Batch #CS12GS: For further information contact Gareth Stevens, New York, New York at 1-800-542-2595.

Contents

- -

Contenido

A farm where pigs live is called a piggery.

Los cerdos viven en una granja porcina.

Pigs are very smart!
They can learn tricks.

¡Los cerdos son muy
listos! Los cerdos pueden
aprender trucos.

A pig can come
when a person calls
its name.

Los cerdos responden
cuando se los llama por
su nombre.

Pigs talk to each other!
They use sounds
called grunts.

¡Los cerdos se
comunican entre ellos!
Los cerdos hacen un
tipo de sonido llamado
gruñido.

A mother pig is a sow.
Baby pigs are piglets.

Las cerdas mamás
se llaman puercas.
Sus bebés son los
cochinillos.

Pigs roll in the mud
to stay cool.

Los cerdos se revuelcan
en el lodo para
mantenerse frescos.

A pig sleeps
on top of straw.

Los cerdos duermen
sobre la paja.

Pigs eat corn.
A farmer feeds them
every day.

Los cerdos comen
maíz. Los granjeros
los alimentan todos
los días.

A pig has 44 teeth!

¡Los cerdos tienen
44 dientes!

Some pigs have straight tails. Some have curly tails.

Algunos cerdos tienen colas rectas. Otros tienen colas enroscadas.

23

Words to Know/
Palabras que debes saber

straw/
(la) paja

tail/
(la) cola

teeth/
(los) dientes

Index / Índice

24